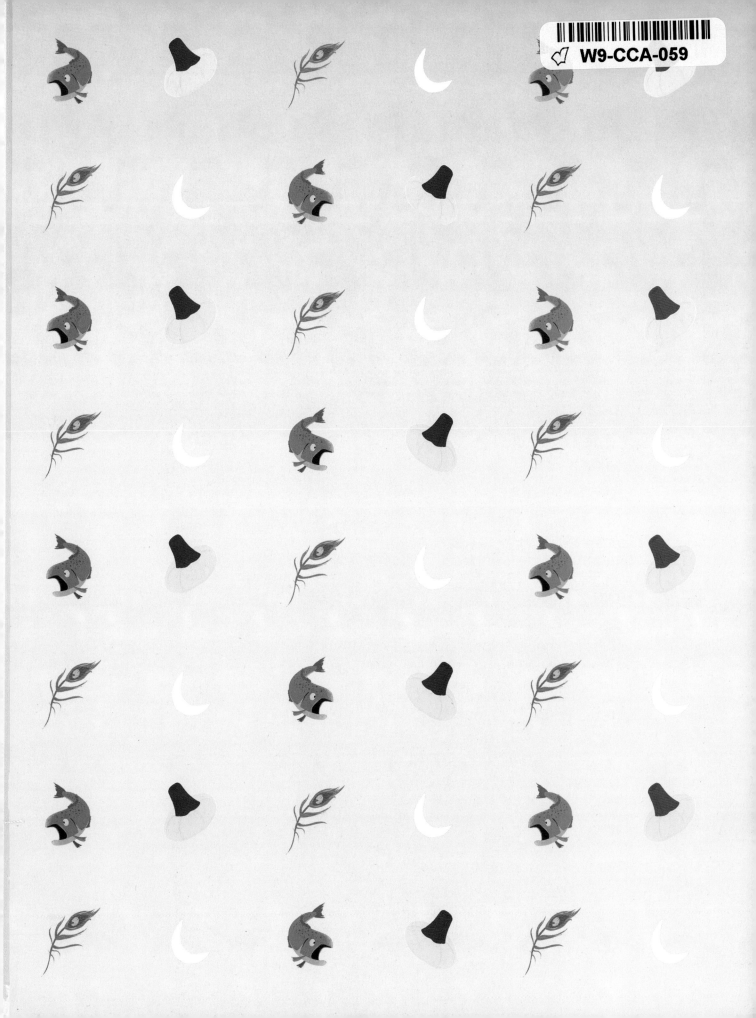

First published in the UK in 2021 by Green Bean Books
c/o Pen & Sword Books Ltd
47 Church Street, Barnsley, South Yorkshire, S70 2AS
www.greenbeanbooks.com

Paperback edition: 978-1-78438-652-8
Harold Grinspoon Foundation edition: 978-1-78438-683-2

Designed by Nathalie Eyraud
Additional art direction by Sammy and Jack Marcus Leventhal
Edited by Kate Baker, Julie Carpenter, Jill Burrows, and Phoebe Jascourt
Production by Hugh Allan

Printed in China by Printworks Global Ltd, London and Hong Kong
072133K1/B1680/A7

In the
Market
of Zakrobat

Based on a tale of Yosef Moker Shabbos

Written by Ori Elon
Translated by Shira Atik
Illustrated by Menahem Halberstadt

This is an ancient folk tale from the land of Babylon.
The story, which comes from the *Gemara**, is about a rich man
and a poor man, a dream and a hat, a fish and a diamond.

* A rabbinical commentary on the Mishnah

In the town of Zakrobat, beside the Euphrates River, a rich man named Baltosar lives alone in a giant fortress. Hidden in his tallest tower are twelve locked chests, all filled with gold coins!

Every morning, he eats
a single bowl of white rice.

Every afternoon, he eats
another bowl of white rice.

And every evening? He takes twelve peas
and eats them with even *more* white rice!

Baltosar never invites guests to his fortress, and he never buys gifts for anyone. "It's true that I have lots and lots of gold," he likes to boast, "but that's because I am very careful with my money!"

Ask anyone in Zakrobat and they'll tell you, "Baltosar's not just careful, he's stingy!"

NO VISITORS!

From his tower, Baltosar can see the hut of his neighbour Yosef – a penniless cobbler with no shoes of his own.

He is known to all as Yosef Moker Shabbos – Yosef who cherishes Shabbat. Why? Because every Friday he walks through Zakrobat Market with his little daughter, Zohar, and asks each and every person the same questions:

"Are you selling anything magnificent today? Fresh fruit, a tasty fish, a pretty flower? A royal visitor is coming tonight. Her name is Shabbat, and she is very dear to me. Do you have something beautiful I can welcome her with?"

All week long, Yosef works from morning to night mending shoes. But on Fridays, when Shabbat draws near, he stops to prepare his feast. Everyone knows that Shabbat dinner at Yosef and Zohar's home is the best in Zakrobat!

Meanwhile, in his tower, Baltosar eats his peas and rice. The sounds of tuneful singing and the aromas of tasty foods rise from Yosef's table and float into the fortress.

"What is he so happy about?" fumes Baltosar. "He's just a penniless cobbler!"

One night, after huffing and puffing with rage, Baltosar finally falls asleep. He soon drifts into a strange dream in which a shiny yellow slide appears just below his window. He imagines his treasure chests sprouting little feet and running, shoeless, onto the slide.

Wheeeee! Down they go!

They giggle as they whoosh along the slide, through an open window, and straight into the hut of Yosef Moker Shabbos.

"Aaaahh!" Baltosar wakes up in horror, his scream echoing through the empty streets of Zakrobat. "I won't have it!" he says, grumpily. "I'm the only one who's allowed to enjoy **my** treasure. Nobody else. And especially not Yosef! I must keep my precious gold safe . . . but what can I do?"

Baltosar comes up with a plan. Early the next
morning, he trades all his gold coins for a single diamond
the size of an ostrich egg.

When he is sure no one is looking, he sews the diamond into the lining of his purple hat. With all his wealth safely hidden on top of his head, he leaves Zakrobat.

Congratulating himself on his
clever plan, Baltosar walks across
the bridge over the Euphrates River.
Suddenly, a storm rolls in.
The wild wind whistles around
Baltosar's head, snatches his hat,
and sends it soaring through the air
like a flying saucer!

"Aaaahh!" he yells, watching
helplessly as his hat lands
on the water and floats away.

As his hat drifts out of sight, Baltosar realises he has lost all his treasure. But, instead of crying, he starts laughing.

"I may not have my diamond or my gold coins," he thinks to himself, "but at least they will never end up in the hands of that cobbler with no shoes of his own!"

Meanwhile, in the depths of the Euphrates
River, a big orange fish swims through
the water, minding her own business.
Suddenly, she sees something extraordinary:
a sparkling egg lying on a purple hat.

"Mmmm,
delicious!"

Back in Zakrobat, life carries on as before, except that Baltosar has disappeared. He has travelled down a far-away river and has made a fresh start in a far-away town.

As for Yosef, he continues to mend shoes from morning 'til night. Another week goes by. On Friday, in the market, he asks each and every person the same questions:

"Are you selling anything magnificent today? Fresh fruit, a tasty fish, a pretty flower? A royal visitor is coming tonight. Her name is Shabbat, and she is very dear to me. Do you have something beautiful I can welcome her with?"

"What about this fish?" asks Zohar.

"I promise you won't be disappointed," says the fishmonger.

And he isn't!

Green
Bean
Books

Look out for these other Green Bean Books!